STARTING RIDING

Helen Edom

Designed by Mary Cartwright and Maria Wheatley

Illustrated by Norman Young

Consultant: Jane Pidcock B. H. S. A. I.

Contents

First things

This book shows how to ride a pony safely while it is walking, trotting, cantering and even jumping. You can learn how to make the pony understand what you want it to do. Later in this book, you can also find out how to care for a pony.

What to wear

Dress in comfortable clothing and sturdy shoes or boots. You also need a crash hat to stop you from hurting your head if you fall off.

Shoes or boots must have a thick heel.

Most riding schools can lend you a hat like this for your first lessons.

Warm-up suits are easy to move in.

Wear gloves to keep from getting blisters on your hands.

This strap goes under your chin.

Saddles and bridles

A pony wears a saddle and a bridle to make it easier to ride. The saddle is like a leather seat on its back.

This saddlecloth, or blanket, makes the saddle more comfortable for the pony.

Saddle

The bridle is buckled around the pony's head. You use the bridle to steer the pony.

Bridle

Neckstrap

There is a stirrup on each side.

This is called the bit. It goes inside the pony's mouth.

This strap is the girth. It fits around the pony's middle.

These long straps are the reins.

Ponies may also wear a neckstrap. You can hold this to help you keep your balance.

2

Going up to a pony

Find out the pony's name first, if you can. Say the name quietly and go up to the pony's shoulder. Move steadily so you do not surprise or frighten the pony.

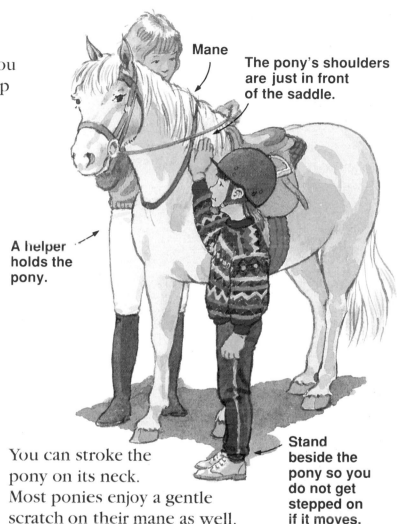

Mane

The pony's shoulders are just in front of the saddle.

A helper holds the pony.

Stand beside the pony so you do not get stepped on if it moves.

Being safe

Always walk around the front of ponies, not behind them. This is because ponies may kick with their back legs if they are startled.

Ponies can only kick you if you are behind them.

You can stroke the pony on its neck. Most ponies enjoy a gentle scratch on their mane as well.

Different colors

Ponies come in all sorts of colors. Here are some to look out for.

Palomino ponies have a gold body and a white mane and tail.

Dapple-grey ponies are white with silver markings on them.

Piebald ponies have black and white patches all over them.

How to get on

Getting on a pony is called mounting. At first it is easier if someone helps to push you up. Later, you can learn to mount the pony by yourself.

Before you mount

First, slide your fingers under the girth. If the girth feels loose, ask for help to tighten it so it holds the saddle firmly in place.

Girth

This should be a tight squeeze.

Now get the stirrups ready. These are on loops called stirrup leathers.

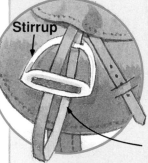

Stirrup

Loop tucked behind stirrup.

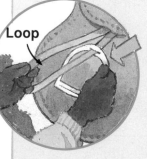

Loop

Take the end of the loop from behind each stirrup. Slide the stirrup down to the bottom.

Taking a leg up

This is the easiest way for someone to push you up. Begin by facing the pony's left shoulder.

Hold the reins in your left hand. Rest this hand on the pony's neck. Put your other hand on the front of the saddle.

Bend your left knee so the helper can hold your leg. He counts to three, then pushes you up.

Swing your right leg over the pony's back so you land gently in the saddle.

Hold some mane as well as the reins.

Move your right hand off the saddle as you land.

Mounting by yourself

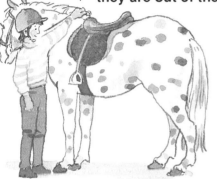

Push the ends of the reins over the neck so they are out of the way.

Stand beside the pony's left shoulder with your back to its head. Pick up the reins as before.

Turn the stirrup toward you with your right hand. Place your left foot inside the stirrup.

Put your right hand on the front of the saddle. Hop around on your right leg so you face the saddle.

Now spring off your right leg and pull yourself up. Stand on the stirrup with your left foot.

Swing your right leg over the saddle. Try to land gently so you do not hurt the pony's back.

Tall ponies

It is easier to get on tall ponies if you stand on a sturdy box or a hay bale.

5

Sitting on a pony

When you begin to ride, a helper leads the pony. This means that you can learn to sit safely without worrying about steering.

Getting your feet into the stirrups

Lift your knees and turn in your toes so you can push your feet inside the stirrups

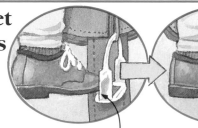

Try to push in your toes without looking down.

The stirrup goes on the widest part of your foot.

Sitting comfortably

Sit in the middle of the saddle. Let your legs hang loosely so their weight rests in the stirrups.

Bend your elbows so your hands are just above the pony's neck. Try riding like this before you pick up the reins.

Sit up so your head, hips and heels are all in a straight line.

Hip

The helper holds the pony with a strap called a leading rein.

Your heel is slightly lower than your toes.

Knotting the reins
While you are learning how to sit, knot the reins like this to keep them out of the way.

Feeling safe
If you feel wobbly, hold on to the neckstrap or the saddle.

Neckstrap

Moving the stirrups

You can move the stirrups if they feel too long or too short.

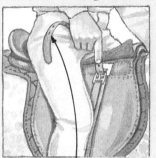

Hold the end of the leather like this. Pull the leather up and free the buckle with your finger.

The stirrup leather has lots of holes for the buckle.

Slide the leather up or down until the stirrup feels comfortable. Try to do this with one hand.

Keep your foot in the stirrup.

Fasten the buckle into the nearest hole and tuck the end of the leather under your leg.

Make sure the leather is flat so it doesn't rub your leg.

Test your balance

Try these balancing exercises while someone holds your pony.

One hand at a time, stroke the pony's neck. See how far you can reach.

Use both hands to touch your knees, toes, and then the back of the saddle.

Stretch out your arms and turn so that one hand points at the pony's ears and the other at its tail. Then turn back to try it the other way.

Keep your legs still.

7

When the pony walks it moves one leg at a time. You can feel a slight bump as each leg moves.

You do not need the reins while someone is leading you.

You should feel comfortable, not stiff.

Sit quietly, trying to make yourself as tall as you can. This helps both you and the pony to feel comfortable.

If you move around or lean forward, like the rider above, the pony will find you awkward to carry.

Try to keep your balance even when the pony stops or starts. Hold the neckstrap whenever you feel unsteady.

Famous walker

Tennessee Walking Horse

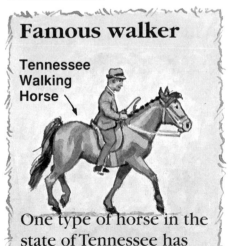

One type of horse in the state of Tennessee has such a smooth, fast walk that it is known as the Tennessee Walking Horse.

Improving your balance

When you feel ready, ask to try some of these exercises while the pony is walking along.

See if you can touch your hands together behind your back. Then touch your head and knees.

Now try swinging your arms in circles. Move one arm at a time, at first. Then use both arms together.

Holding the reins

When you can keep your balance really well you can learn to hold the reins.

Unknot them and pick up each side with your thumb on top like this.

The ends of the reins hang down the pony's neck.

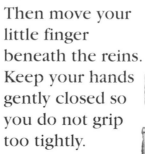

Then move your little finger beneath the reins. Keep your hands gently closed so you do not grip too tightly.

Make sure your hands are level.

Always remember that the reins go to a metal bit inside the pony's mouth. You can hurt the pony if you tug at the reins.

Metal bit

Riding in a school

It is safest to start to ride in a fenced-off area called a school. A teacher, called a riding instructor, stands in the middle and tells you what to do.

On the lunge

Sometimes the instructor holds your pony with a long line, called a lunge rein. She uses it to make your pony go around her in a circle.

Lunge rein

Practicing at home

You can practice picking up the reins with a piece of string at home. See how quickly you can get your fingers in the right place.

Going wherever you want

You can give signals to a pony with your voice, legs and hands. These tell the pony what you want it to do. When you can give clear signals you can ride by yourself.

Asking your pony to start

Keep the rest of your body still.

Nudge like this.

Nudge the pony's side with both heels when you want it to start or to walk faster. It helps to say "walk on" firmly.

Take care not to pull back on the reins as the pony starts to move. Say "good pony" as soon as the pony obeys.

Shortening reins

It is hard to give clear signals if your reins are too long. Shorten them like this.

This hand stays still.

This hand pulls.

The rein slides through.

Use the thumb and first finger of one hand to pull the rein up through the other hand.

Asking your pony to stop

Never pull for very long.

The reins make the bit press on the pony's mouth.

Sit up tall and close your legs briefly on the pony's sides. Move your hands back to tighten the reins.

Loosen the reins then try again and again until the pony stops. It also helps to say "ha-aalt" calmly.

Turning the pony

When you turn, keep your pony moving steadily by nudging with both heels.

Turning left

To turn left, squeeze your left hand on the rein and move it out a little. Let your other hand go forward as the pony turns its head.

Move your right hand out to turn right. Be careful to sit straight, looking where you want to go.

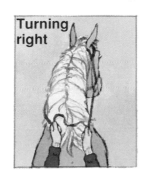

Turning right

You could practice turning your pony in and out of a line of plastic pots or cones.

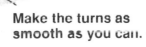

Make the turns as smooth as you can.

Secret steps game

This game will help you practice your skills. First, the riders line up while a helper marks a line some distance away. The helper then turns his back and counts aloud.

The helper stands behind the line.

You may need help to steer your pony at first.

The riders get their ponies to walk as far as they can before the helper reaches ten. On "ten" the helper turns around and anyone still moving goes back to the start. This goes on until someone wins by crossing the line.

Trotting

When a pony trots, it moves its legs two at a time. This makes trotting feel much bumpier than walking.

Sitting trot

At first, when you trot, someone leads you so you can just sit still and hold the saddle. Try to count "one-two, one-two" in time with the bumps.

Rising trot

Trotting is easier if you rise up and down. Practice rising when the pony is standing still. Lean slightly forward and push into the stirrups to lift your bottom off the saddle.

Knot the reins to keep them out of the way.

See if you can move up and down with your arms folded.

Use the neckstrap to help you.

Be careful not to pull on the reins.

Then try rising when the pony is trotting. Count "one-two" again, in time with the bumps. Rise on "one".

Sit when you say "two" but get ready to rise again as soon as your bottom is in the saddle.

When you can rise up and down steadily, you can hold the reins so you can steer the pony.

Going from walk to trot

You need shorter reins when you trot because the pony holds its head higher. Shorten them just before you ask the pony to trot.

Then nudge the pony's sides with both heels and say "trot on" briskly. Sit for the first few bumps, then begin to rise.

Walking again

Sit for a few bumps and close your legs briefly on the pony. Say "wa-aalk calmly. Move your hands to tighten and loosen the reins until the pony begins to walk.

Trotting maze

When you can trot steadily, you can have fun practicing steering. Ask a helper to place plastic pots in pairs like this.

Use your legs to keep the pony going while you guide it with your reins.

See if you can make your pony trot between each pair. Go back to the beginning if you miss any out.

Trotting races

Some horses are trained to trot very quickly. They go in trotting races, pulling a light cart.

The driver uses extra long reins to steer the horse.

How to get off a pony

Here you can find out how to get off and lead a pony safely. Getting off a pony is called dismounting. Make the pony stand still before you begin.

First, take both feet out of the stirrups. Then hold the reins in your left hand.

Rest your left hand on the pony's neck. Put your right hand on the front of the saddle.

Now lean forward and swing your right leg over the saddle.

Keep your hand on the reins as you land on the ground by the pony's side.

Running up the stirrups

Before you lead your pony away, run up the stirrups like this to stop them banging against the pony's side.

Still holding the reins, slide the stirrup up the leather loop.

Push the stirrup up the lower side of the loop.

Tuck the loop through the stirrup. Do this to both stirrups.

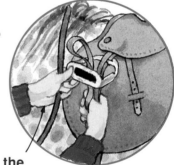

Keep hold of the reins all the time.

When you finish, both stirrups should look like this.

Leading the pony

Stand on the pony's left side and pull the reins over its head. This makes it easier to lead the pony.

Hold both reins close to the pony's mouth with your right hand. Pick up the ends with your left hand so you do not trip over them

Stay beside the pony's shoulder.

Never wind the reins around your hand as you cannot let go quickly if you need to.

This is wrong.

Say "walk on" to the pony. Begin to walk and the pony should walk beside you. Say "ha-aalt" calmly and stand still when you want it to stop.

Musical sacks

Play this game with your friends and an adult helper. You also need a radio and some sacks.

The players must run up their stirrups before leading the pony.

The helper puts down a sack for each player except one. The players ride around while the helper plays the music.

When the helper stops the music everyone gets off and leads their pony to a sack. Anyone without a sack is out.

Another sack is taken away and the rest ride around again. This goes on until only one player is left who wins the game.

Better riding

It takes a lot of practice to become a good rider and make your pony do what you want all the time. Here are some tips to help you when you have lessons.

School movements

The instructor uses special commands to tell everyone what to do. "Go large" means go around the school.

If you go around to the left you are "on the left rein". If you go to the right you are "on the right rein".

On the left rein, all the turns are to the left.

On "change the rein", everyone turns across the school, one behind the other. Then they go along the track the other way.

Using a riding whip

When you can ride well you can carry a riding whip. Hold the whip so it rests across your leg.

If ever your pony ignores your leg signals, take the reins in one hand.

Use your other hand to smack the pony once with the whip, just behind your leg.

This reminds the pony to obey your signals.

For "turn in and halt", everyone turns their pony off the track and stops in a line.

Things to remember

Sit quietly, remembering to keep your head, hips and heels in a straight line.

Use the signals you have learned to keep the pony moving steadily.

This is a safe distance.

These ponies are too close.

Push with the leg on the inside of the bend.

Steer carefully around the corners. You can stop your pony cutting them by pushing its side with your leg.

Always keep a safe distance from the pony in front. This pony might kick out if you get too close.

Look out for letters

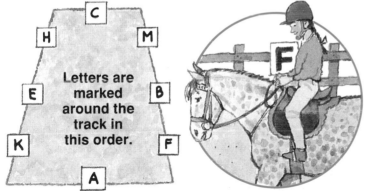

Letters are marked around the track in this order.

C

H   M

E   B

K   F

A

There are usually letters marked around the track. If the instructor tells you to do something at a letter, give signals to

your pony in plenty of time. See if you can get your pony to obey just as your shoulders are level with the letter.

Riding clothes

Here are some clothes you can buy if you want to do a lot of riding. You can often get them secondhand from a riding school.

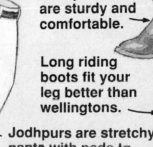

Jodhpur boots are sturdy and comfortable.

Long riding boots fit your leg better than wellingtons.

Jodhpurs are stretchy pants with pads to keep them from getting worn out.

Cantering

When you are good at steering your pony in a trot, you can learn to canter.

Cantering is faster than trotting but it feels much smoother.

Asking your pony to canter

Begin a canter at a corner of the school. Make your pony trot steadily up to the corner.

Outside leg

Try to relax your back.

Your leg moves back this far.

Your outside leg returns to its usual place.

Stop rising as you begin to turn. Move your outside leg back slightly and nudge it against the pony's side. Say "canter" firmly.

The pony seems to rock forward and back as it canters. Sit up and let your hands move so you do not pull against the pony.

How the pony moves

The leading leg is in front of the others when it is on the ground.

When a pony canters, the hoof beats come in sets of three. First the pony puts down one back leg.

Then the pony puts down its other back leg together with a front leg on the opposite side.

Lastly, the pony puts down its other front leg. This one is called the leading leg.

Trotting again

Your hands only move a little way.

It is easiest to get your pony to trot along a straight side of the school. Close your legs briefly and say "tro-ot" calmly. Tighten and loosen the reins until the pony trots.

Disobedient ponies

Sometimes a pony may just trot faster when you ask it to canter. If this happens, slow down and try again at the next corner.

A difficult pony may canter more easily if you ask it to canter just as it goes over a pole.

The instructor puts the pole across a corner.

Keeping steady

It is easier just to canter a few steps at a time until you get used to it.

The outside hand is the one nearest the side of the school.

To begin with, you can hold both reins in your outside hand. Then you can hold the saddle with your other hand.

Swinging your legs

You can practice moving one leg by itself while the pony is walking.

Hold the reins in one hand.

Take your feet out of the stirrups. Lift up each stirrup and cross the leathers in front of the saddle.

Now, swing one leg at a time backward and forward from the knee. See if you can keep the other leg still.

Jumping

When a pony jumps, you can feel it stretch out its neck and spring upward and forward. It is easier to keep your balance if you bend forward as the pony jumps. This is called the jumping position.

Practicing the position

You can practice the jumping position while the pony is standing still. Keeping your back straight, lean forward from your hips. Push your heels down at the same time.

Your bottom may slide back in the saddle.

Your knees rest against the saddle.

Try this without reins, at first.

If this seems difficult, shorten your stirrups by one or two holes and try again.

Going over poles

Try walking and trotting over a pole on the ground. Go into the jumping position over the pole.

Move your hands forward.

Steer straight for the middle of the pole.

Keep rising as you go over.

The pony stretches out its neck as it steps over the pole. Push your hands toward the pony's mouth so the reins do not pull the pony back.

Your instructor may put a few poles in a row. Try to hold your position while the pony trots over them all.

20

A small jump

Ride straight for the middle of the jump.

When you are good at going over poles you can trot your pony over a small jump. Bend forward slightly but keep your bottom in the saddle as you go up to the jump.

Show jumping

In show jumping competitions, people ride over a course of colored jumps.

The poles fall down easily if they are touched.

They try to jump over all the fences first time, without knocking any of them down.

Your bottom may come just out of the saddle.

Keep your back flat.

Keep your heels down.

As the pony takes off, bend forward a little more. Push down with your heels to help keep your balance.

Look straight ahead but let your hands go forward as the pony stretches out its neck over the jump.

As you land, begin to sit up again. Get ready to steer the pony where you want to go next.

Games and outings

As you become a better rider you can have fun doing different things with your pony.

Riding outside

Leading rein

Riding in the open is called hacking. At first, someone can lead you from a horse to help you control your pony.

If you go on a road, keep in to the side so cars can pass you. It is safer and more fun to ride along tracks or fields instead.

Riding clubs

You can join a riding club. These have meetings for lessons and games.

Some clubs have fancy dress competitions like this.

Ask at your riding school to find out about a club near you. If you get stuck, try writing to some of the addresses on page 32.

Greedy ponies

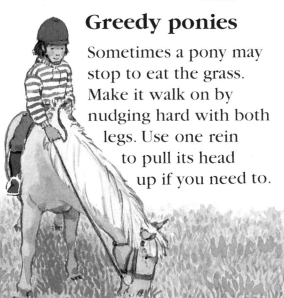

Sometimes a pony may stop to eat the grass. Make it walk on by nudging hard with both legs. Use one rein to pull its head up if you need to.

Grass reins

Extra straps, called grass reins, can be fastened between the bridle and the saddle. They keep the pony from putting its head down to eat grass.

Gymkhanas

You can enter games competitions at local horse shows. These are called gymkhanas. This is what you have to do in some of the games.

Flag races

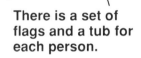

Starting by a tub, you race to a set of flags. Pick up one flag at a time and drop it in the tub. The winner is the first to move all their flags.

There is a set of flags and a tub for each person.

Giving treats

When you are pleased with your pony you can give it an apple or a carrot as a treat. Many ponies also like mints.

Slice carrots lengthways so the pony does not choke.

Hold the treat with your hand flat like this. The pony takes the food gently with its lips.

Bending races

Each pony goes up its own line of poles.

You steer your pony in and out of a line of poles. Turn around the last pole and race in and out back to the start.

Sack races

Hop as fast as you can.

Everyone races their pony to a line of sacks. You get off and get into a sack. Then you lead your pony back to the start.

Rosettes

If you are lucky you may get a rosette for being first, second or third. Even if you are last, do not forget to pat your pony for trying.

In the stable

Most ponies live in a stable for part of the day. The rest of the time they go out in a field so they can eat grass.

A pony's stable

Some stables have long rows of compartments called stalls. A pony can be tied up in each one.

Other stables are like small rooms. These are called loose boxes because the pony can be let loose inside them.

The dirt is taken away in a wheelbarrow.

Straw makes the ground comfortable to stand on. Dirty straw and droppings are taken out every day.

What a pony eats

Ponies eat other food besides grass. Here are some things they can eat or drink.

Hay is dried grass. It is stuffed into nets which are tied up in the pony's stable.

Ponies need clean water near them all the time.

Oats are like porridge oats but with the husks still on.

Bran comes from wheat.

Pony nuts are made of chopped up grass and cereals.

Ponies become ill if they eat too much, so never give any food unless you have asked a grown-up first.

Catching a pony

When you want to lead a pony out of a field you need to use a headcollar like this one. Carry it into the field with you.

Head-strap

Leading rope

Do up the noseband before you go near the pony.

Ask a grown-up to help you at first.

Call the pony's name and walk calmly up to its shoulder. Loop the rope over the pony's neck.

The noseband goes about half-way up the nose.

Hold the rope if the pony moves away.

Slip the noseband over the pony's nose. Then fasten the headstrap just behind the pony's ears.

Now take the rope off the pony's neck so you can lead the pony to its stable.

Tying a pony up

Most stables have a metal ring on the wall. You can tie your pony up to a string loop fixed to this ring. Use a knot that you can quickly undo.

String

This goes to the head-collar.

Ⓐ Ⓑ

Push the leading rope through the string. Make the rope into a loop.

Ⓑ Ⓐ

Take side A over side B and back down behind the loop.

Ⓐ Ⓑ

Pull just some of side A through. Pull side B to tighten the knot.

Pull here to undo.

You can undo the knot by pulling hard on the free end of the rope.

Grooming

Ponies need to be brushed to keep them clean. This is called grooming. Before you begin, tie the pony up so it stands still.

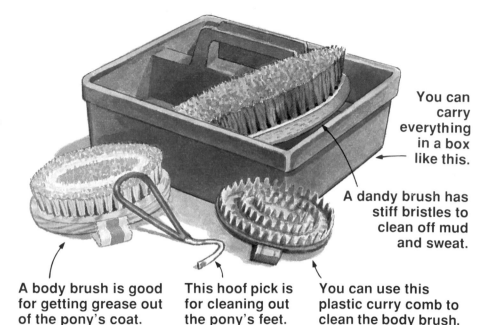

You can carry everything in a box like this.

A dandy brush has stiff bristles to clean off mud and sweat.

What to use

Here are some things you need to groom a pony. When you first use them, ask your instructor to help.

A body brush is good for getting grease out of the pony's coat.

This hoof pick is for cleaning out the pony's feet.

You can use this plastic curry comb to clean the body brush.

Using a hoof pick

A pony's foot, or hoof, is hollow so dirt gets trapped inside. Here you can see the underneath.

Heel

This soft part is called the frog.

Most of the inside is hard horn.

Toe

This metal shoe keeps the hoof from getting worn down.

Start at the very top of each leg.

Be careful not to dig the hook into the frog.

Hold the foot firmly.

Ask the pony to lift up each foot by running your hand down its leg and saying "up".

Run the hoof pick from the heel to the toe, beside the frog, to get the dirt out.

Brushing a pony

Before you start, look for lumps or cuts. Tell a grown-up if you find any.

You can sweep the brush to and fro.

Push the curry comb away from you like this.

Rub off the mud and dried sweat with a dandy brush. This brush is scratchy so do not use it on the pony's head.

Use the body brush in long strokes all over the pony's body. Hold the curry comb in the other hand.

Every so often, clean the brush by rubbing the comb against it.

Be very careful not to hurt the pony's eyes or nostrils.

Stand to one side while you brush out the tail.

Waterproof coats

Many ponies live outside at night. Natural oils in their coat help to keep out the rain.

Use the body brush by itself to brush the head. You can hold the pony's nose to keep its head still.

Brush the mane and tail with the body brush. Brush a few hairs at a time to get out all the tangles.

These ponies are groomed lightly so as not to brush out too much oil.

Tacking up

Putting on a saddle and bridle is called tacking up. This takes lots of practice so ask someone to help you while you learn. Tie the pony up before you start.

Putting on a saddle

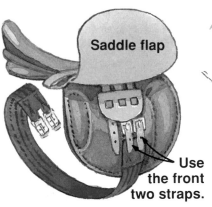

Saddle flap

Use the front two straps.

First, lift the flap on the right side of the saddle. Make sure that one end of the girth is buckled to the straps underneath.

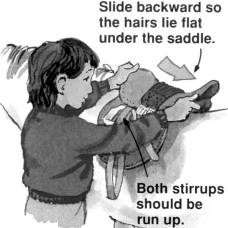

Slide backward so the hairs lie flat under the saddle.

Both stirrups should be run up.

Loop the girth over the saddle and go to the pony's left side. Lift the saddle onto the pony's shoulders and slide it into place.

Western saddles and bridles

Many people still ride with the same kind of saddles and bridles that cowboys used. This is called riding Western-style.

The reins are held in one hand.

Go around the front of the pony so you can lift the girth down. Let it hang and go back to the left side.

Use the front straps again.

Now pick up the end of the girth. Buckle it onto the straps underneath the left saddle flap.

Keep your hand flat.

Run your hand under the girth to make sure that it is not pinching the pony's skin. Do this on both sides.

Putting the bridle on

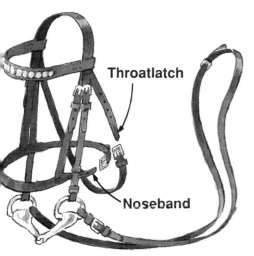

Throatlatch

Noseband

First of all, make sure that two of the buckles are undone. These are on the straps called the noseband and the throatlatch.

Undo this buckle on the headcollar.

Go to the pony's left side. Put the reins over the pony's head so they rest on its neck. Then undo the headcollar and slip it off.

Keep your fingers outside the pony's mouth.

Rest the bit on your left hand. Open the pony's mouth by pressing the corner with your thumb. Guide the bit gently inside.

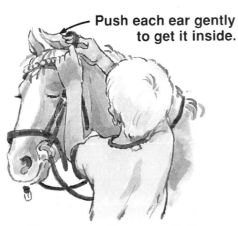

Push each ear gently to get it inside.

Now put the top of the bridle over the pony's ears. Smooth out any bits of mane that get trapped under the bridle.

Then do up the buckle on the throatlatch. The throatlatch fits loosely so you can get your hand inside like this.

Finish off by doing up the buckle on the noseband. The noseband should be just loose enough for you to get two fingers inside.

Untacking

Taking off the saddle and bridle is called untacking. Lead the pony into its stall or box before you untack it. You also need to have its headcollar handy.

Taking off the bridle

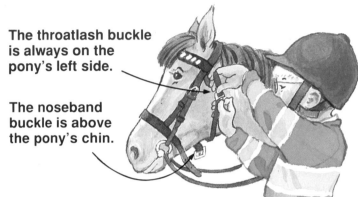

The throatlash buckle is always on the pony's left side.

The noseband buckle is above the pony's chin.

First undo the buckle on the noseband. Then undo the buckle on the throatlash.

Rest your hand on the pony's nose to stop it raising its head.

Now lift the top of the bridle and carefully push it over the pony's ears.

Do not let the bit bang the pony's teeth. This hurts a lot.

Hold the bridle in your right hand while you slide the bit gently out of the pony's mouth.

You can hold the pony with the reins if it tries to walk off.

Now rest the bridle on your shoulder while you put on the pony's headcollar (see page 25).

Lift the reins high over the pony's ears.

Put your hand on the pony's nose if you need to.

Finally, take the reins over the pony's head. Loop them on your shoulder while you tie the pony up.

Taking off the saddle

Put the bridle in a safe place while you take off the saddle. Start by lifting up the left saddle flap and undoing the girth.

Undo both of the buckles.

Keep hold of the girth so it does not fall and bang the pony's leg. Lower it carefully so it hangs without swinging.

Now go around the front of the pony. Pick up the girth on the other side and loop it over the saddle.

Put one hand on the front of the saddle and one on the back. Slide the saddle off the pony.

Putting the saddle and bridle away

Remember to take the saddle and bridle away and hang them up. You can carry them like this.

Saddles go onto long flat stands. Bridles are hung on round pegs.

If you need to put the saddle down for a moment, before hanging it up, stand it on its front like this.

Index

Useful addresses

British Equestrian Centre,
Stoneleigh, Kenilworth,
Warwickshire,
CV8 2LR,
England.

American Horse Show Association Inc.,
220, East 42nd St,
Suite 409 New York,
NY 10017, USA.

New Zealand Equestrian Federation,
P.O. Box 47,
Hastings, Hawke's Bay,
New Zealand.

Canadian Equestrian Federation,
1600 James Naismith
Drive, Gloucester,
Ontario,
K1B 5N4,
Canada.

Equestrian Federation of Australia Inc.,
40, The Parade,
P.O. Box 336,
Norwood,
S. Australia, 5067.

First published in 1992 by Usborne Publishing Ltd, Usborne House, 83-85 Saffron Hill, London, EC1N 8RT, England. Copyright © 1992 Usborne Publishing Ltd.

Printed in Belgium. AE